PLEASE WASH
YOUR HANDS
BEFORE YOU READ ME
AND KEEP ME CLEAN

Career Day

story by **Anne Rockwell** pictures by **Lizzy Rockwell**

HarperCollins*Publishers*

Visit our web site at http://www.harperchildrens.com. • Library of Congress Cataloging-in-Publication Data • Rockwell, Anne F. • Career day / story by Anne Rockwell ; pictures by Lizzy Rockwell. p. cm. Summary: Each child in Mrs. Madoff's class brings a visitor who tells the group about his or her job. ISBN 0-06-027565-0. — ISBN 0-06-027566-9 (lib. bdg.) [1. Schools—Fiction. 2. Occupations—Fiction.] I. Rockwell, Lizzy, ill. II. Title. PZ7.R5943 Car 2000 97-20999 [E]—DC21 CIP AC Typography by Elynn Cohen 1 2 3 4 5 6 7 8 9 10 ❖ First Edition

For Christian and Sam,

who will grow up to do something wonderful.

—A.R. and L.R.

When special visitors come to our school,
they tell us about the work they do.
Then we tell them about the work we do.
Today it's my turn to introduce my visitor.

Jessica
CALENDAR
Sam
JUICE
Michiko
LEADER
Charlie
LIGHTS
Nicholas
WEATHER
Kate
PLANTS
Eveline
SNACK
Pablo
FLUFFY
Evan
Sarah
MAIL

What if I forget what I'm supposed to say?
Sometimes that happens.
Not just to me, Mrs. Madoff says,
but to everyone.

Here he is—right on time!
"Uh, this is my dad," I say.
"He drives a big bulldozer.
He's helping build our new library."
"Good morning, Mr. Lopez," everyone says.
"Good morning, boys and girls," my dad says.

Next we meet Charlie's visitor.
His mother is a judge who works
in a courtroom and wears a long black robe.
If there's too much noise, she pounds her gavel
and says, "Order in the court!"
Then everyone has to be quiet.

When Kate introduces her visitor, she says, “My dad plays bass in an orchestra at night. He practices all day and takes care of my baby brother while our mother goes to work at the bank.”

Michiko's mother writes books for us to read.
She draws the pictures in them, too.
She is very good at drawing mice.

Mrs. Madoff's visitor is her husband.
He's a scientist called a paleontologist.
He just got back from South America,
where he was digging for dinosaur bones.
The bones tell us about dinosaurs
that lived long ago.

Sarah's visitor is our crossing guard.
She brings Sarah to school every day,
because she is also Sarah's grandmother.
That's why Sarah is always the first one at school
and the last one to go home in the afternoon.

STOP

Eveline's mother is a nurse in the hospital.
She takes care of all the newborn babies in our town.
She tells us those babies are very, very cute,
but they sure do cry a lot when they're hungry.

GIRL
BRION
8lb. 3oz.

Jessica's mother takes care of animals. She's a veterinarian, the kind of doctor who makes sick animals better.

Sam's visitor drives the sanitation truck
that carries our garbage to the big town dump.
Kate and Eveline and I wave to him, just as
we always do whenever he comes down our street.
"Hey, kids—remember to recycle!" Sam's father says.

Evan’s father wears a leather apron
that holds the tools he uses all the time.
He shows us how to hammer a nail.

When it's time for Nicholas
to introduce his visitor, he says,
"I'll bet you've all bought groceries
at the Friendly Farm Market.
Guess what—my father is manager of the store."

Friendly Farm Market
SPECIAL!
Farm Fresh Eggs
MELONS
$1 EACH
$5
$2 BAG
APPLES
APPLES

Grown-ups sure have interesting work to do!
And so do we.

I wonder what I'll be when I grow up.

TICKET

Today it's Mr. Siscoe's turn
to introduce his special visitor.
He says, "Good morning, everyone.
I'd like you to meet Professor Alcorn.
He's my teacher at college."
Hey—I never knew grown-ups
had teachers, too!

Piaget
Ch. 10 - 15
Test Monday